75

ACROSS THE STREAM

BY MIRRA GINSBURG

PICTURES BY NANCY TAFURI

Julia MacRae Books

First published in the United States of America 1982
by Greenwillow Books
First published in Great Britain 1983 by
Julia MacRae Books, a division of Franklin Watts
12a Golden Square, London W1
Printed in Belgium

British Library Cataloguing in Publication Data
Ginsburg, Mirra
    Across the stream
    I. Title
    813′.54[J]   PZ7
    ISBN 0–86203–113–3

Across the Stream was inspired
by a verse of Daniil Kharms

To
Raphael &
Eva & Peter
With Love
M.G.

To
Ava
Susan & Libby
With
Gratitude
N.T.

A hen

and three chicks

6

had a
bad
dream.

They ran and came

9

to a
deep,
wide
stream.

The hen
said, "Cluck,
we are
in luck.

I see three ducklings

and a duck."

The duck was kind,
she did not mind.

16

She said, "Quack, get on my back."

They were in luck.
They crossed the stream –

a chick on a duckling,

18

a chick on a duckling,

19

a chick on a duckling,

and the hen on the duck.

And what became of

the bad dream?

It was left on the other side of the stream.